SPIDER- ™

HOW TO DRAW

by Michael Anthony Steele
Illustrated by Mada Design, Inc.

SCHOLASTIC INC.

New York   Toronto   London   Auckland   Sydney
Mexico City   New Delhi   Hong Kong   Buenos Aires

ISBN 0-439-65080-1

Designed by Maria Stasavage

Published by Scholastic Inc.
SCHOLASTIC and associated logos are trademarks and/or registered trademarks of Scholastic Inc.

12 11 10 9 8 7 6 5 4 3 2 1   4 5 6 7 8/0

Printed in the U.S.A.
First printing, May 2004

ARE YOU READY?

Then let the *Spider-Man 2* adventure continue!

Keep the fun and excitement of *Spider-Man 2* alive and spinning by drawing your very own scenes from the hit film! This book will offer step-by-step instructions on following basic drawing techniques, creating dramatic backgrounds, and drawing several of the main characters from *Spider-Man 2* — including the amazing webslinger himself, Spider-Man!

So get your pencil ready and prepare to help Spider-Man fight crime and protect the city as you learn how to draw *Spider-Man 2*!

As you follow along with the instructions inside, remember that not all the characters in Spider-Man's world are the same exact height. Don't forget to check the size chart below to make sure that Mary Jane doesn't look taller than Doc Ock, for example!

Mary Jane   Peter Parker   Spider-Man   Dr. Otto Octavius   Doc Ock

BASIC DRAWING TIPS

You'll find that most things you draw are made up of basic shapes. They might be hard to see sometimes, but they are there. As you draw the *Spider-Man 2* characters in the following pages, you'll start with basic shapes like squares, triangles, circles, and ovals.

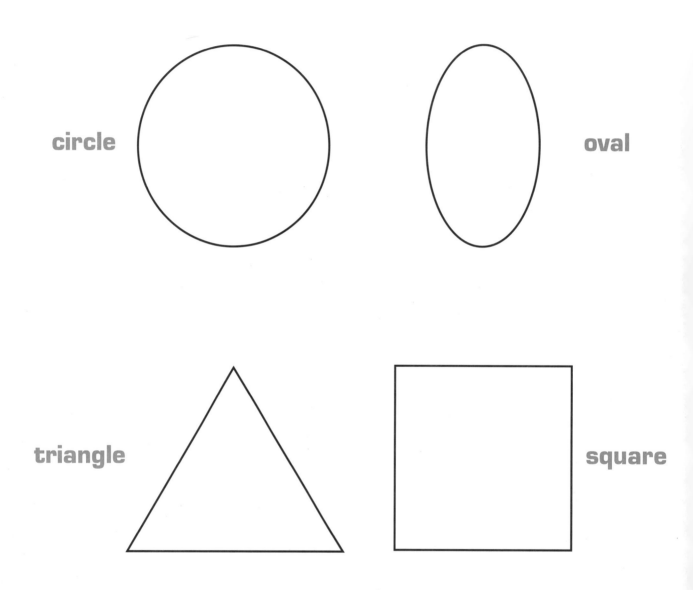

circle

oval

triangle

square

YOU WILL NEED:

- Paper
- An eraser
- Sharpened pencils
- Colored pencils, markers, or crayons
- Pencil sharpener
- A ruler

Next, you'll turn those basic shapes into three-dimensional or 3-D objects. This means they will look as if they have length, depth, and width instead of looking flat.

3-D objects can be drawn with "dotted lines" representing the lines defining the back or inside of the object. See how quickly a plain square can become a cube? And a triangle can quickly become a cone.

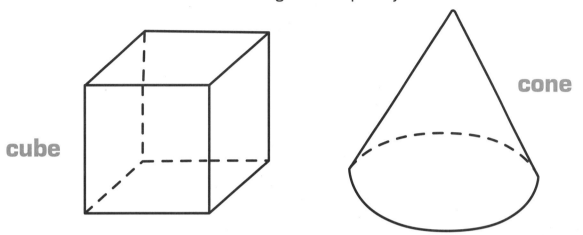

cube

cone

The two objects below also look 3-D, but there are no dotted lines representing the lines we can't see. This is because of *shading*.
Once you've drawn an object, you can add depth by choosing where an imaginary light source shines upon it, then add a shadow to the opposite side. This is probably easiest with a colored pencil (or a regular pencil for a black-and-white drawing). Simply press harder on the darkest part of the object (where the shadow is) as you color the drawing. Press more lightly as you move across the surface of the object until you reach the light side.

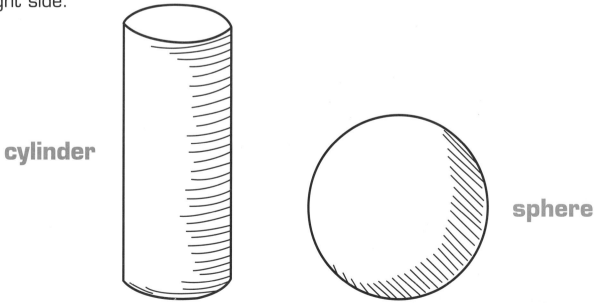

cylinder

sphere

See how there appears to be a light shining just to the left of the cylinder and sphere?

SPIDER-MAN'S MASK

Let's start with Spider-Man's famous mask. When criminals see this mask, they know it won't be long until they're strung up in a web, waiting for the police to arrive.

STEP 1

Draw an oval for the shape of Spider-Man's head. Then *lightly* draw a vertical line (from top to bottom) down the center of the oval. Don't worry if the line isn't completely straight — you'll erase it later. Now draw a horizontal line (from left to right) through the center of the oval. This is where the webslinger's eyes would be. Place a small dot where the two lines meet.

NOTE: The eye line is usually drawn halfway down a face.

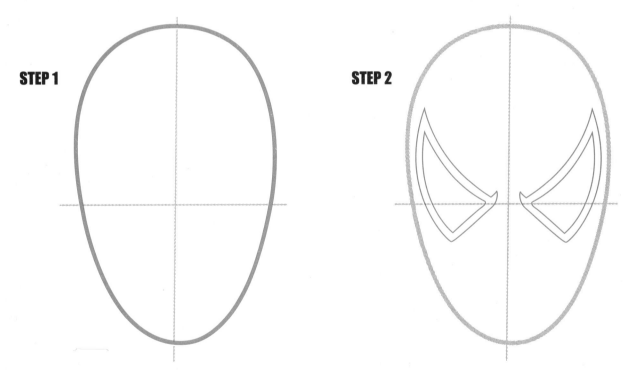

STEP 2

Draw Spider-Man's eyes. Use the horizontal line to position the eyes and to keep them even with each other.

GENERAL NOTE: As you can see in this image, the lines drawn for this particular step are blue. This way you can tell the difference between what you just drew and what you're going to draw next.

STEP 3

Erase the horizontal and vertical lines, but keep the dot in the center. Now begin drawing the web on the front of Spider-Man's mask. Remember, the webslinger's face isn't completely flat, so be sure to add a small curve to these lines. The curves suggest the shape of Spider-Man's face under the mask.

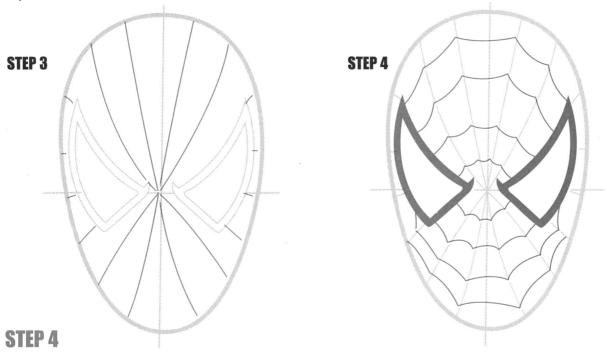

STEP 3

STEP 4

STEP 4

Now finish the drawing by filling in the border around Spider-Man's eyes. Then complete the webbing on his mask. In reality, spider webs droop a bit, so don't just draw straight lines connecting the webs — add a slight curve to them.

SPIDER EMBLEMS

Get ready to draw the famous spiders from the front and back of Spider-Man's costume!

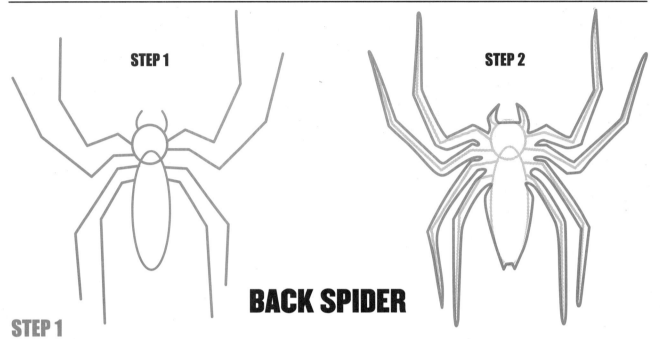

STEP 1

STEP 2

BACK SPIDER

STEP 1
Draw a circle for the spider's head and an oval for the spider's body. Then lightly draw lines representing the spider's legs and jaws.

STEP 2
Using the lines as a guide, draw an outline around the spider. Don't its jaws seem creepier? Now erase the lines you drew earlier. This spider is from the back of Spider-Man's costume and is colored red.

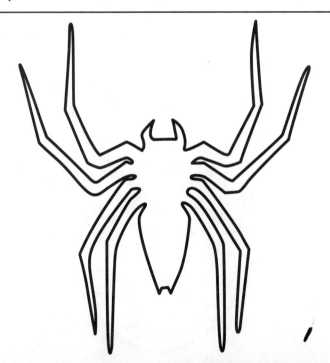

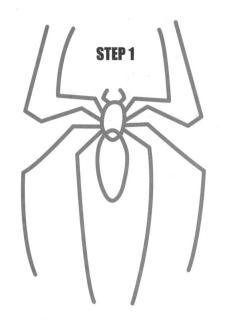

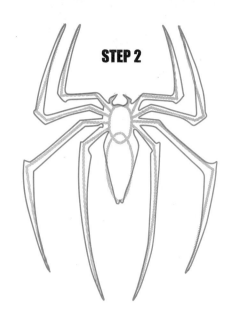

FRONT SPIDER

STEP 1

As with the first spider, begin by lightly sketching basic shapes for its head, body, and legs. Remember, feel free to sketch as many lines as you want until you get the perfect shape. Later you can erase the lines that don't fit.

STEP 2

This spider is different. Notice how the joints of its legs widen to a point, giving it a spooky look. This spider is colored completely black and is on the front of Spidey's costume.

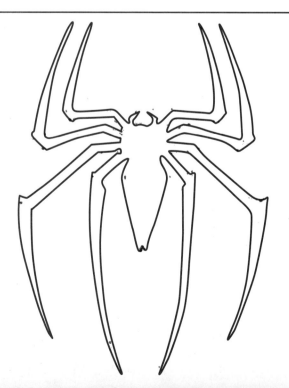

WEBSLINGING ACTION!

Now it's time to go 3-D! After Peter Parker was bitten by that genetically altered spider, he discovered he could shoot webs from his wrists. Get ready to practice drawing 3-D objects by drawing Spider-Man's web-shooting wrist!

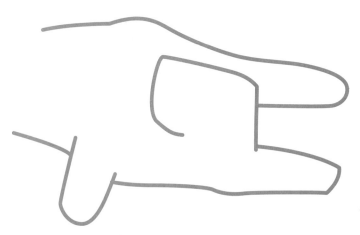

STEP 1

As with most drawings, start by lightly sketching the general position and shape of the object. This helps get the image from your head to the paper. Maybe the image doesn't turn out exactly how you pictured it in your mind. This way you can continue sketching until the general shape matches what you were thinking.

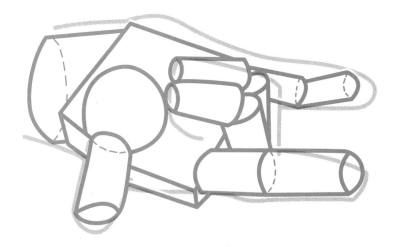

STEP 2

Once you're satisfied with the basic shape, add some of the 3-D objects from pages 4 and 5. See how Spider-Man's hand is made of a flat box, a sphere, and several cylinders?

GENERAL NOTE: Be careful not to focus *too* intensely on your drawing. Always glance back and forth from your work to the object you're drawing.

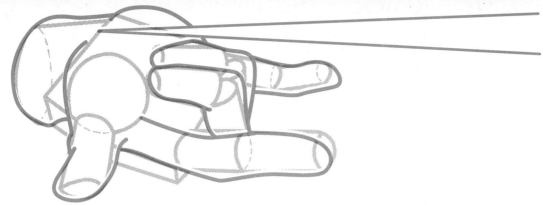

STEP 3

Now darken the lines that best define the drawing you're trying to create. Once you have the image you're after, erase the lines that don't fit. Use your ruler to create a web shooting from the webslinger's wrist.

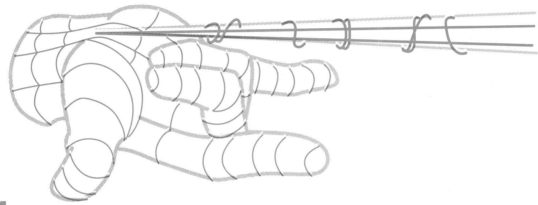

STEP 4

Add the details of Spider-Man's glove. Don't just draw straight lines — imagine the shape of a real hand when you draw in the curving lines. The web he's shooting isn't just a bunch of straight lines either. Add several smaller webs that wrap around the main ones.

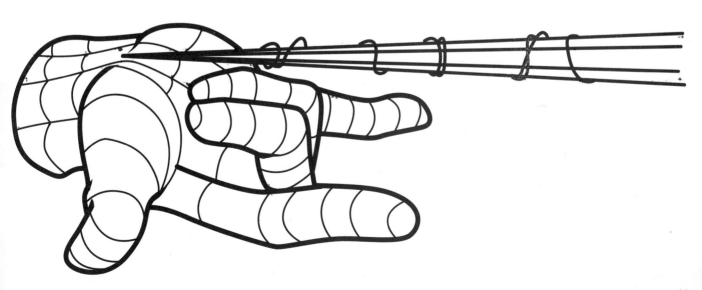

GREAT POWER!

When Peter Parker wears his Spider-Man costume, he's ready for anything. It's time to draw the webslinger as he prepares to spring into action!

STEP 1

Just like our bodies have skeletons, sometimes it's easier to begin a drawing with a simple framework. Using basic shapes, draw Spider-Man's pose. Draw an oval for his head and then use crossed lines to represent the direction he's looking. Draw a large circle for his chest and a smaller oval for his hips. Notice how his arms and legs bend using smaller circles for elbows and knees. The hands and feet are drawn using ovals or close to oval shapes.

STEP 2

Sketch out 3-D shapes to give your drawing depth. Notice how one large cylinder replaces the sphere in the chest and the sphere of his hips. The arms and legs are broken into cylinders that meet at the elbows and knees.

NOTE: Be sure that the objects closer to you (like Spider-Man's two feet) are larger than the ones further away. This is a form of *perspective*. It adds depth and realism to a drawing.

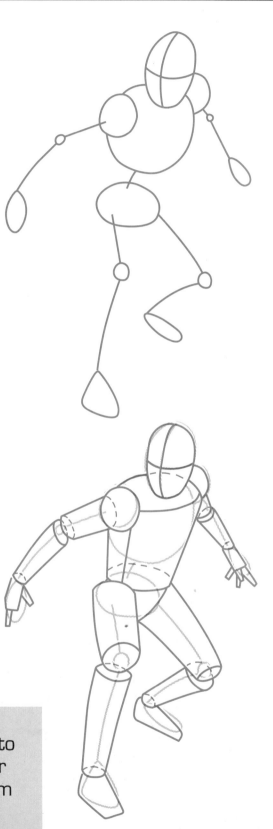

STEP 3

Darken the lines you wish to keep and erase the ones you don't need. Add the webslinger's eyes. Add lines defining the main pattern of his costume.

STEP 4

Now it's time to add the details. Draw the webbing on Spider-Man's mask and costume. Add the spider from earlier in the book. Just don't draw it flat as you did before. Be sure to give it a little perspective as well.

CRAWLING THE WALLS

This is why some call him the wallcrawler! Draw Spider-Man climbing down a building, ready to pounce on the bad guys!

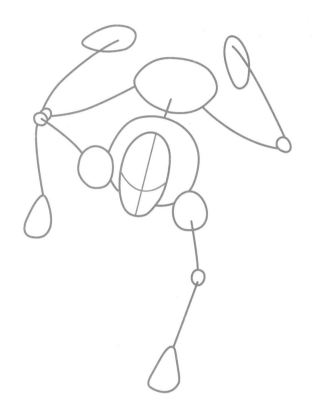

STEP 1

Start with the basic framework that defines the final pose. This time, draw Spider-Man's head almost completely overlapping the oval of his back. His leg lines also overlap his oval feet.

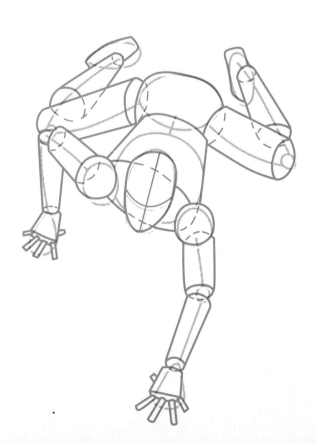

STEP 2

Add 3-D shapes to your drawing. Use the basic shapes, but notice how they overlap differently in this pose.

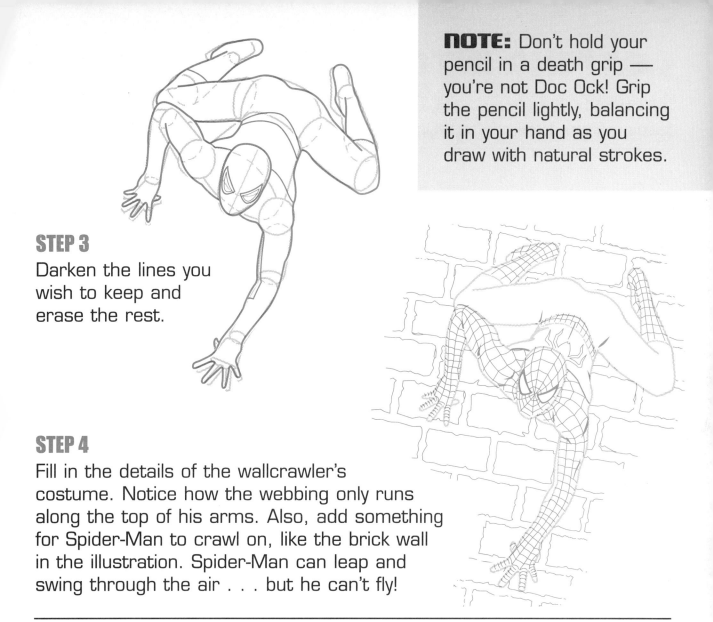

STEP 3

Darken the lines you wish to keep and erase the rest.

STEP 4

Fill in the details of the wallcrawler's costume. Notice how the webbing only runs along the top of his arms. Also, add something for Spider-Man to crawl on, like the brick wall in the illustration. Spider-Man can leap and swing through the air . . . but he can't fly!

LEAPING INTO ACTION

Whether he's dodging a blow from one of Doc Ock's deadly arms or leaping from a tall rooftop, Spider-Man is often in this classic pose.

STEP 1

Sketch in the framework. Spider-Man's arms are almost completely straight, but his legs are bent sharply at the knees.

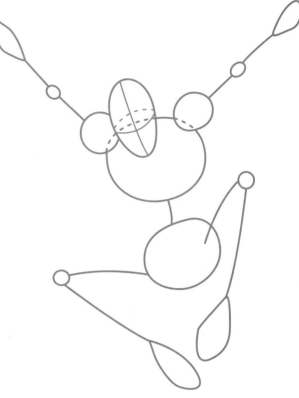

STEP 2

As you add the 3-D shapes, notice that the cylinders representing his shins almost hide the rest of his legs.

STEP 3

Spider-Man's chest muscles tighten as he spreads his arms wide. His eyes look down slightly, toward his point of attack.

STEP 4

As before, fill in the webbing and add the spider emblem.

JUST HANGING AROUND

Sometimes the best way for Spider-Man to spy on an enemy is to slowly descend on a strand of webbing.

STEP 1

Drawing Spider-Man in this pose begins the same as any other time — except that the framework is upside down!

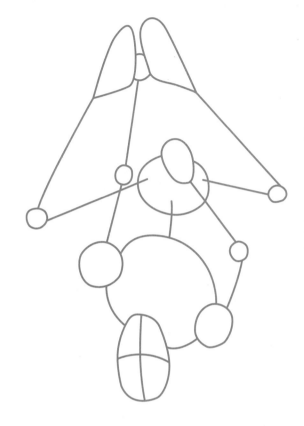

STEP 2

The webslinger's knees are bent sharply and his arms are positioned to grip the web.

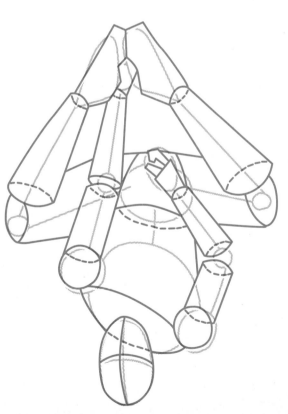

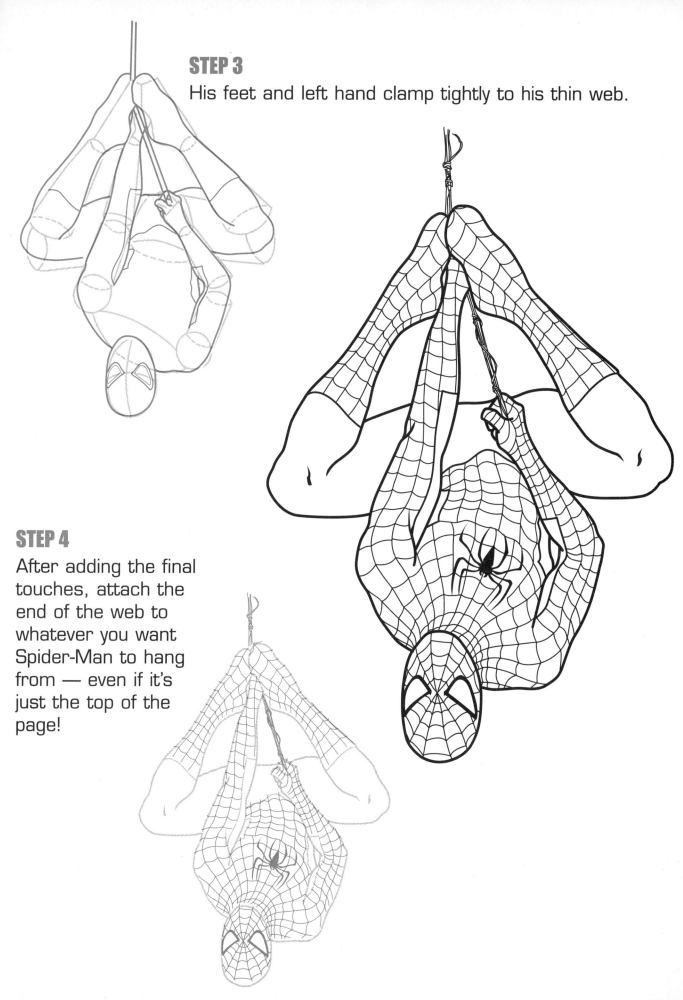

STEP 3

His feet and left hand clamp tightly to his thin web.

STEP 4

After adding the final touches, attach the end of the web to whatever you want Spider-Man to hang from — even if it's just the top of the page!

DON'T MESS WITH DOC OCK!

Caught in a freak laboratory accident, the brilliant scientist Dr. Otto Octavius turns into Doc Ock! With his highly advanced robotic arms, this evil genius has stunning power to back up his dangerous schemes!

STEP 1

Start with a framework of Doc Ock's arms spread wide and legs bent in a defiant pose.

STEP 2

Add larger 3-D shapes to Doc Ock's form. The evil scientist isn't as lean and muscular as Spider-Man, so make them big.

STEP 3

Once the basic shape is drawn, add Doc Ock's familiar trench coat. Now erase the part of his body that won't be seen under the coat.

STEP 4

While adding the final details, be sure to include Doc Ock's scowl and mussed hair. Oh . . . and don't forget the four bone-crushing metal arms!

COME INTO MY LABORATORY

This is the laboratory of Dr. Otto Octavius. Here is where the doctor's smart arms experiment went horribly wrong. The accident fused the robotic arms to his spine, turning him into the multi-tentacled Doc Ock. Use this drawing as a guide to draw your own laboratory or cut out your

drawing of Doc Ock and place him onto this one. Then you can add your drawing of Spider-Man and have an epic battle between the hero and villain!

BEHIND THE MASK — PETER PARKER

When Spider-Man isn't swinging from the rooftops, he is Peter Parker — college student and photographer for the *Daily Bugle*.

STEP 1
Standing in a bit of a slouch, Peter Parker's hands are raised to take a photograph.

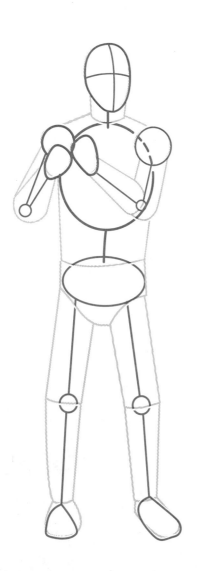

STEP 2
Use larger 3-D objects to form Peter's body. His baggy jeans and shirt hide his muscular body — and his Spider-Man costume!

STEP 3

Erase the unused lines and define Peter's shoes, jeans, and shirt. Use the eye line on his face to position his eyes.

STEP 4

Add the final details including his shoelaces, camera strap, and folds in his clothes.

HOME SWEET HOME

It doesn't look like the secret hideout of a world-famous superhero, but to Peter Parker, this is home.

Use this drawing as a guide to draw your own version of Peter's apartment. Or you can cut out your drawing of Peter Parker and place him onto this one.

THE GIRL NEXT DOOR

Peter Parker has had a crush on Mary Jane since they were both six years old. Mary Jane is starting to develop deeper feelings for him as well. Will Peter let her know about his true feelings?

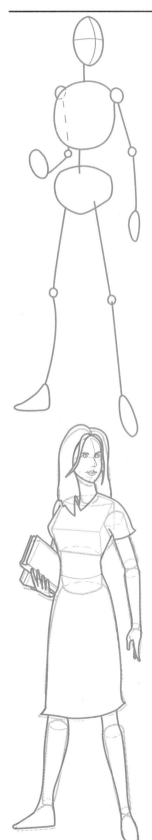

STEP 1

No stranger to the stage, Mary Jane stands straight and proud. Her right arm is bent to hold a couple of stage plays.

STEP 2

Along with the other 3-D shapes, add the outline of her hair as well as the shape of her dress.

STEP 3

Add MJ's facial features, along with a couple of loose strands of hair. Define her blouse, skirt, and hands.

STEP 4

Add the finishing touches on Mary Jane's shoes, the pattern on her blouse, and the seam on her skirt.

SPIDER-MAN AND THE CITY

It would be difficult for our hero to swing from skyscrapers and leap from rooftop to rooftop without an actual city around him! Sharpen your pencil and get your ruler ready as you prepare to add some dramatic backgrounds to your *Spider-Man 2* drawings.

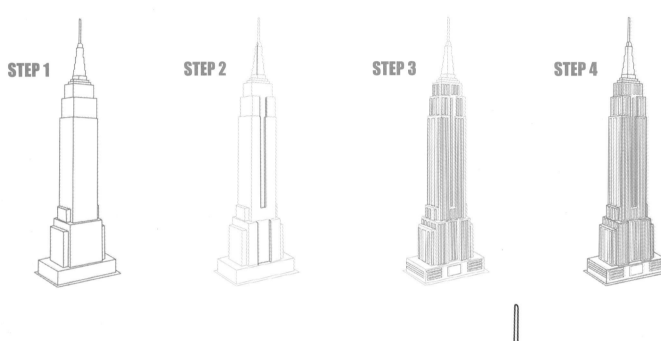

STEP 1   **STEP 2**   **STEP 3**   **STEP 4**

SKYSCRAPER

Although this may seem more difficult, drawing this 3-D skyscraper is just like drawing a tall 3-D box. The angled lines give this building depth just like the previous 3-D objects. Just be sure to use your ruler so all of the lines are straight. Notice how the horizontal lines near the top of the building are not as angled as the ones near the bottom. This makes the building seem taller and more realistic.

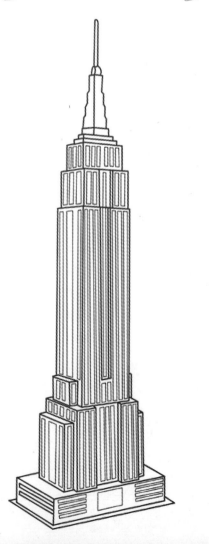

CITY SKYLINE

In a big city, buildings come in all different shapes and sizes. Some are tall and thin. Some are short and fat. Some buildings have rounded roofs, while others have flat ones. Some have many tiny windows while others have just a few large windows. Let your imagination go wild as you create your own city skyline. Just use your ruler, start with simple shapes, and fill in the rest as it comes to you.

WITH GREAT POWER COMES GREAT RESPONSIBILITY!

And with a little time and patience, you'll soon have the webslinger swinging through the city, protecting the innocent! It will help if you follow the instructions and copy the illustrations in this book exactly at first, but once you've got the basics down, don't be afraid to create your own scenes. The sky's the limit!

STEP 1

STEP 2

STEP 3

STEP 4

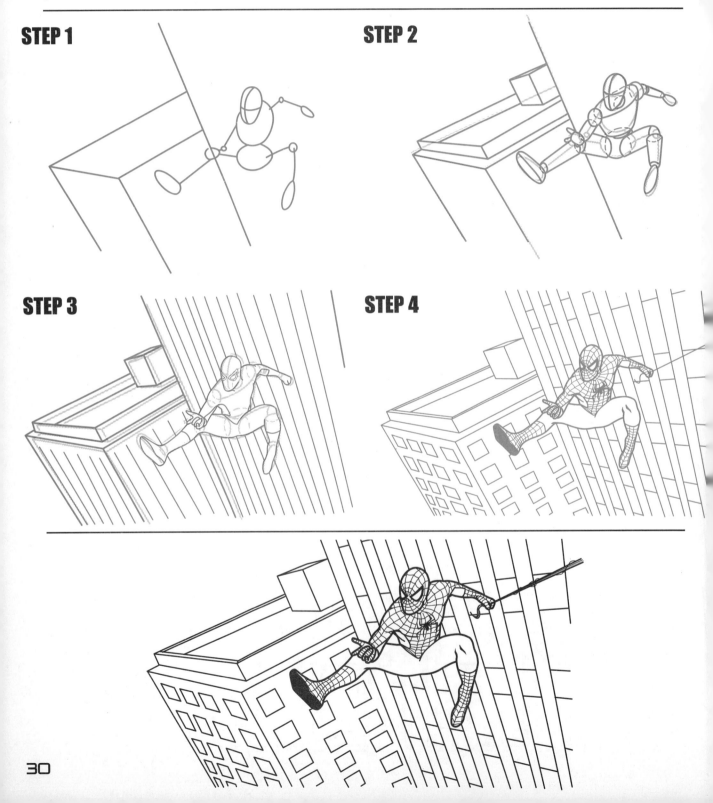

PRACTICE MAKES PERFECT!

The more you practice your drawing skills, the better you'll become. Soon you'll be able to draw Spider-Man and Doc Ock battling it out anywhere you can imagine!

SPIN A WEB, ANY SIZE . . .

What better way to end this book than to show you how to draw Spider-Man's calling card — his spider web. When you see this web, you know that your friendly neighborhood Spider-Man was there.

STEP 1

Make a dot in what will be the center of the web. Next, use your ruler to draw straight lines from the dot to where the web will end. For a more realistic look, don't draw a straight line perfectly through the dot. Just draw a line from the edge to the dot, then move the ruler slightly and continue drawing the line from the dot to the opposite edge.

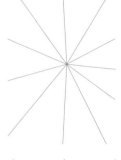

STEP 2

Starting at the center, draw smaller lines across the long lines you just finished. Keep them realistic by adding a small curve to them as you go. Spiral them all the way out to the edge of your web.

STEP 3

No web is perfect. Add a few smaller webs that cross the others.

STEP 4

For a finishing touch, thicken the main webs a bit. Then add a few smaller ones spiraling around different parts of the entire web.

Now get out there and start drawing heroic characters and exciting scenes from the smash hit *Spider-Man 2!*